THE COOKIE SHOP

ALEXANDRIA BLAELOCK

Also by Alexandria Blaelock

SHORT STORY COLLECTIONS
The Histories of Hayward Hall
Lovelorn, Lovestruck and Love at First Sight
Common or Garden Variety Heroes
Case Files of the Wilkinson Detective Agency
Unavoidable Fates
Christmas Travesties
Five Faces of Felicia Clarke
Little Place Called Home

FICTION
That Love Nonsense
Taipan vs Brown
The Ghost and Ms Cox
Friends Like That

MS BLAELOCK'S BOOKS
Stress Free Dinner Parties
Signature Wardrobe Planning
Holistic Personal Finance
Minimally Viable Housekeeping
Planning a Life Worth Living

A SELECTION OF AVAILABLE SHORT STORIES
Alma's Grace
Fate in Your Hands
Lady of the Looking Glass
Morning Star, Evening Star, Superstar
Secret Singer
Shining Star
Ship in a Bottle
Simone Says Hands in the Air
The Day the Schedule Broke

THE COOKIE SHOP

ALEXANDRIA BLAELOCK

BlueMere Books
MELBOURNE, AUSTRALIA

For permission requests, please contact enquiries@bluemerebooks.com.

Ordering Information:
Discounts are available on quantity purchases. For details, contact orders@bluemerebooks.com.

The Cookie Shop/Alexandria Blaelock
paperback ISBN: 978-1-923083-01-1
digital ISBN: 978-1-923083-02-8

Book Layout © BookDesignTemplates.com
Cover Art © grandfailure/Depositphotos

THE COOKIE SHOP

Imagine the most wonderful room you can. For some, it's gleaming glass and steel, or stained teak and red leather. Or maybe you'd prefer a garden room with cypress hedges enclosing a wildflower meadow.

Whatever you can imagine, the Cookie Shop is better than that.

Children line up outside its windows looking in, comparing notes about what they can see; racks of jars of boiled sweets, shelves of cakes, or, in my case, live birds tearing each other to pieces.

Though of course they're children and you can't rely on them for accurate and factual reporting, can you?

What we do know is that as you age, what you see in the window changes.

You might see shelves of books, racks of different coloured yarns, or in my case, jars of preserved scientific specimens.

It's a mystery how the room knows what you need to see.

And no one knows how it can be possible that two people standing right next to each other can see completely different things.

But somehow, it just happens like that.

No one knows exactly where the shop came from either, or why there's only one in State City. Or why you have to visit it at least once every five years until the door opens for you, and then never again.

Why some-five-year-olds walk right on in, but Mr Jonas Quinn died at age ninety-seven without ever having gained entrance.

There are lots of theories, of course; God, the devil, body snatching worms, brainwashing communists, possessive ghosts, and mind sucking aliens.

To name just a few.

Not that it matters, at some point 99.999% of people have no choice but to enter.

Because when the door opens, you can't escape it.

And just as children see different things when they look in the window, so the people who gain entry come out with different stories about what happened when they went inside.

Even though no more than one person at a time is allowed inside, some see other people (or creatures posing as people), while others see no one. Not even someone who explains what's happening.

All we know for sure is that when the door finally opens and at last you walk inside, you get a delicious cookie.

And you can't leave until you've eaten it.

I, Yohanna Lalami, expect it's a bit like one of those magical shops that turns up for a day so you can buy that thing you need and then disappears overnight, never to be seen again.

Except without disappearing overnight.

Or getting that thing you need.

Or maybe it's not like that at all.

But one thing is for sure, everything changes once you eat your cookie.

Though no one can tell you how, or why.

Except those who knew you before say there's something different about you, even if they can't say what it is.

But it seems for some, it's pretty big because they move away and are never seen or heard of again.

Not to mention those who go in, but don't come out again.

It's like some weird arse rite of passage, like your first period, or sexual experience with another person, or a drug or alcohol-induced life-threatening hangover.

I tried my whole life to stay away from the Cookie Shop. I can't say why, but it made me feel uncomfortable.

Or maybe I can.

I don't like being told what to do, so there was no way I was going to willingly go past it.

Or maybe it was just those birds.

Except, of course, circumstances always conspired against me, and I'd be in the City on a School Trip, and naturally we had to walk past it. Or when I was at university, and my work experience placement was right next door.

And now, here I am again because my boss sent me into the City to deliver some papers to a supplier. I've no idea why - email would have been quicker and more reliable than me.

But I bet if I ask him, he won't be able to come up with a reasonable explanation.

The Cookie Shop does that to you.

Nothing about it ever makes sense until after you've eaten your cookie and are back outside.

Like somehow, even though I walked in completely the wrong direction, I ended up standing in front of the Cookie Shop.

And even though I turned my back and walked away, I ended up coming back around to it from the opposite direction.

And while I was there, the door opened invitingly.

Even waggling a little in encouragement.

I tried backing up and away from the door, but some interfering old biddy took up a cry that the door was open, and that I was refusing to enter, and led a commotion to push me, struggling all the way, through it.

Interfering old biddies are just the worst.

So even though I resisted the press of the crowd and clung desperately to the door frame, I found myself on the wrong side of the closed door.

It was all stunning silence, white light, and the smell of lightning.

Not too hot, and not too cold.

And for all that, not really substantial enough to be any of those things.

Except for the hundreds of thousands of millions of little blue lights that spun and danced around me, singing or talking or something I couldn't quite hear but that set the hair on my arms standing on end.

I tried to avoid them by crouching low and ducking around the room, but they followed me. Like the flocks of starlings you see at sunset, or a shoal of fish trying to avoid a shark attack.

It seemed a very long time that they circled me.

And every now and again, one single light would veer away from the flock and flicker out.

Ridiculously, the more lights that left me, the more annoyed and angry I got.

How dare they reject me!

I stood tall, brow furrowed, and lips pressed firmly together in the middle of the room. With my fisted hands firmly set against my hips, challenging them to do their worst.

It seemed they were laughing at me, which just made me madder.

You might be wondering why I didn't just wrench the door open and leave.

It's very simple.

The door wasn't there anymore.

After about forever, I couldn't be angry anymore.

It was just too tiring.

So, I lay down on the suddenly soft floor, curled up, and took a nap.

When I woke, there weren't many lights left, maybe a hundred or so.

Few enough to count, though because they were still circling and moving, they were too fast to count properly.

I watched them for a while; they were strangely hypnotic.

But they'd become more like seagulls at the beach competing for chips. Kind of lunging at each other and pushing each other out of the way.

And then as I swallowed, a few of them winked out, which seemed to stir the rest into a frenzy of even greater attack against each other.

I'd never heard of anything like this happening in the Cookie Shop.

Though, again, it is different for everyone.

And in general, most people walked in and then out again almost immediately.

Was I somehow different to most people?

Or did everyone have more or less the same experience because time inside the Cookie Shop somehow took longer than time on the outside?

I took another sip of my drink, and the lights came to rest, watching me again.

They looked the same as each other, just like most seagulls do (aside from the ones missing legs. Or pretending to miss them).

But I was becoming aware of distinct personalities between them, just like you do when you watch the birds for long enough.

The timid one that sits a little further apart from the main group.

The bold one that sits a little closer to you.

The one that stands on one leg tricking you into feeling sorry, so you aim your chips at it.

The loud one that does most of the screeching.

The little one that all the others pick on.

The creepy one that watches you and makes overly familiar eye contact.

They seemed to be grading me.

I twisted around and turned my back on them, but in an instant, a slightly smaller group appeared in front of my face.

I guess I'd lost a few more.

My stomach rumbled again, and they sort of swooped to gut level.

What to eat became a more pressing concern. Something a little creamy to balance the Campari's acidity. Maybe a little salty, with a rich mouthfeel.

Italian, of course, because I was drinking Campari after all.

A nice plate of sage buttered spaghettini, loaded up with Parmesan and freshly ground black pepper.

And there it was.

Which was, of course, about the time I wondered whether it was safe to consume, but decided that seeing as I'd almost finished the drink, I was doomed either way, so I might as well eat.

The little lights seemed to agree and floated back up to eye level. Or maybe mouth level.

I twirled my fork in the pasta to collect a mouthful, and it was as mouthwateringly delicious as I had imagined, though as I closed my eyes in ecstasy, I thought I saw a few more lights wink out.

And when I opened them again, the lights were at each other again.

They were still going hard at it when I finished the pasta and started licking the plate.

I heard the whisper of a buzz at the edge of my hearing.

A buzzing that sounded a lot like a scourge of mosquitoes. I ducked and waved a hand around my head, just in case.

They must be furious if I could hear them.

The plate disappeared, and I finished the drink and watched it disappear too.

Then lay back down, contemplating what to eat next.

A cookie I supposed, given I was in the Cookie Shop.

One of those crispy biscotti, the kind with thin slices of nut you dip into your rich honey flavoured dessert wine?

Or one of those lovely light French Roses de Reims you dunk in your champagne?

Or just a nice plain digestive with a cup of tea?

Argh!

The biscotti were calling to me, and I thought perhaps an espresso would be better off sobering me up when I left the shop.

But it didn't appear.

I was frowning at the air I expected it to appear.

And then I realised there were only three lights left in front of me, jiggling erratically, as if to say "pick me! Pick me!"

As if I had to choose one before I got my Cookie.

And it seemed too important a decision to just randomly grab one, so I looked very hard at them, trying to understand who they were.

And then I put my hands towards them and shuffled them like they were upside down cups with peas in and I was taking bets.

And then I closed my eyes and tried to feel them.

And when I opened my eyes, there were still three there.

Though they weren't jiggling any more, I felt like they were looking at each other. I think one might have shrugged.

I was also a bit tired of the game, so I opened my arms, and closed my eyes, and leaned back, offering them my heart.

I felt a sharp sting in my forehead and blacked out for a moment.

When I came to, there were no blue lights, but there was a plate with a big slice of pavlova topped with cream and fresh berries, along with a small glass of wine.

It was delicious.

As I ate, I tried to figure out what the fuss was all about.

I didn't feel any different...

Actually, that's not quite true. I felt more like me.

Like I was somehow a deeper and more substantial me than before.

Bigger, better, faster. More certain about who I was, and what I was doing with my life.

Though, not really more like me, maybe more than the me I was before.

As I walked out the door, it seemed to me that when I saw the live birds fighting; I was closer to the truth than I realised.

THE END

ABOUT THE AUTHOR

Alexandria Blaelock writes stories, some of them for *Ellery Queen's Mystery Magazine* and *Pulphouse Fiction Magazine.*

She's also written five selfhelp books applying business techniques to personal matters like getting dressed, cleaning house, and feeding your friends.

She lives in a forest because she enjoys birdsong, and the smell of gum leaves. When not telecommuting to parallel universes from her Melbourne based imagination, she watches K-dramas, talks to animals, and drinks Campari. At the same time. Discover more at alexandriablaelock.com.

Why not try *The Ghost and Ms Cox*

Life interrupted

To say the letter was a surprise was an understatement. It arrived addressed to Miss Finlay Cox, which made the contents even more extraordinary.

Orphan Finn Cox inherits a cottage. Thinks it holds the key to her origins. Of course she takes a look. Who wouldn't?

But when she gets there, she gets more than she bargained for.

Is it friend, family or foe?

www.ingramcontent.com/pod-product-compliance
Lightning Source LLC
Chambersburg PA
CBHW061926220726
48287CB00018B/1088